The BDSM Sessions

The BDSM Sessions

Raven Delacroix

Aubrey, Texas. USA

Published by Cathouse Publishing, an imprint of Cathouse Creations
Aubrey, Texas, USA

Print Edition ISBN: 9798998589591
Printed in United States

For permissions, inquiries, or more information, contact:
Cathouse Publishing - cathouse.publishingtx@gmail.com

For K,
the love of my life.

Author's Note

Welcome, dear reader, into my poetic realm—a collection of fifty intimate journeys into the heart of BDSM, where desires whisper, boundaries shift, and the exquisite dance of dominance and submission unfolds. I am Raven Delacroix, and within these poems, I invite you to explore the shadowed corridors of passion, trust, and profound vulnerability.

Each poem is crafted with intent and sensitivity, drawing you into a narrative where pleasure and pain harmonize beautifully, weaving stories uniquely resonant and deeply personal. With every verse, I invite you closer, guiding you through the delicate interplay of power and surrender, control and release. Here, each line becomes a tapestry of emotion, carefully designed to ignite the senses and touch the deepest recesses of your being.

This poetic journey is more than mere exploration—it is transformation. Embrace the intensity, savor the anticipation, and open yourself fully to the captivating experiences captured in these pages. Allow yourself to feel deeply, to crave boldly, and ultimately, to transcend into the thrilling sanctuary of my poetic world.

Yours in trust and passion,

Raven Delacroix

Table of Contents

Consent is King

Before the touch,
before the binding,
before the first whispered command—
there is a moment.
A pause.
A question unspoken,
but understood.

"Do you trust me?"

This is where it begins.
Not with control,
not with pain,
but with choice.
With clarity.
With the power you hold
in the simplest word:
"Yes."

Consent is not silence.
It is not taken.
It is given.
Freely.
It is the line drawn and redrawn,
the map we follow

with every step,
every breath.

It is a conversation—
fluid, constant,
woven into the fabric of everything we do.
Your voice,
my ears.
Your body,
my hands.
Each move a dialogue,
each sound a guide.

Without it,
there is no trust.
Without it,
there is no us.

Consent is not weakness—
it is strength.
It is standing tall,
owning your boundaries,
claiming your desires.
It is the courage to say,
"This is where I begin,
and this is where I end."

And I honor that.
I cherish it.
I build upon it,
because I know
what you give me
is a gift.

The binding?
It is freedom.

The sting?
It is connection.
The surrender?
It is power,
because it is yours to give,
never mine to take.

Consent is not a single moment.
It is every moment.
It is the thread that ties us,
the safety that grounds us,
the fire that fuels us.

Because here,
in this space we've created,
consent is not just a rule—
it is everything.
It is the crown we both wear,
the promise we both keep.
It is the foundation,
the core,
the truth.

Consent is king.

The Dance of Control

It begins with a step.
A movement so small,
you almost miss it.
A tilt of the head,
a lowering of the gaze,
the quiet surrender of space.

You lead.
I follow.
But only because I choose to,
because this is our dance,
and every step,
every turn,
is built on trust.

Your hands find me—
not to take,
but to guide.
Not to force,
but to invite.
Your touch, firm yet careful,
is a question,
and my body answers.

We move together,
a rhythm only we can hear.

Your voice,
low, steady,
is the melody,
and I am the harmony,
rising and falling in time with your words.

It is not a battle.
It is not a fight.
It is a balance,
a perfect tension,
where control is not stolen,
but given freely.

You pull,
and I lean in.
You push,
and I yield.
And in that give and take,
we create something greater
than either of us alone.

The dance changes.
The pace quickens,
and my breath catches,
but I don't falter.
Your grip tightens,
not to hold me back,
but to steady me,
to remind me
that even as I fall,
you are there.

This is not chaos.
This is precision.
Every move calculated,
every step, deliberate.

You test me,
push me,
take me to the edge,
but never beyond.
You know my limits
even when I forget them.

And when the music slows,
when the tension fades,
you don't let go.
Your hands stay,
a quiet reminder
that this dance
is never truly over.

We find stillness together,
breathing as one,
hearts beating in rhythm.
This is not just a dance.
It is a language,
a conversation of bodies,
a symphony of trust and surrender.

And as you guide me back to myself,
your voice soft,
your touch steady,
I know I will follow you again.
Because this dance,
this perfect, unspoken choreography,
is where I belong.

Collared

It is more than leather,
more than steel.
It is a weight I choose to bear,
not as a burden,
but as a bond.

When it circles my throat,
I feel its presence,
cool against my skin,
a reminder—
I am seen.
I am held.

You place it there,
your hands deliberate,
your eyes searching mine for a flicker of doubt.
There is none.
Only the steady hum of surrender,
the quiet roar of belonging.

This is not control taken,
but trust given.
Not a symbol of weakness,
but of strength in yielding,
a declaration that echoes louder than words:
I am yours.

Each link, each clasp,
each subtle tug against my skin
carries meaning,
a language spoken not with tongues,
but with touch.

And when I kneel,
it is not to diminish,
but to rise within this moment,
to stand taller in my submission
than I ever could unbound.

The world fades when I wear it,
narrowing to your gaze,
your hands,
your voice.
I feel the pull of the collar
not as a restraint,
but as freedom
to be fully, unapologetically mine—
and yours.

Collared,
I am not lost,
but found.
Not broken,
but whole.
I wear it proudly,
this circle, this bond,
a crown of devotion
that marks me as more
than I ever knew I could be.

The Weight of Words

It's not the rope that binds you,
not the leather against your skin.
It's the words I speak—
soft, sharp, deliberate—
that hold you still.

Each syllable lands heavy,
not as a command,
but as a promise.
A whisper can become a tether,
a single phrase, a shackle.
And you give yourself to it,
breath by shivering breath.

"*Kneel.*"
Not because you must,
but because my voice pulls you there,
drawing you into the quiet gravity
of surrender.

Every word,
a key,
unlocking the part of you
that only I can reach.
And with every yes,
with every begged "please,"

you tell me—
you trust me to hold the weight
of your desires,
of your fears,
of you.

There is power in silence, too—
the way you wait,
aching for the next word
to shape you,
to break you,
to build you.

Do you feel it?
The way my voice presses into you,
carving into the tender corners of your resolve.
It lingers there,
even when I've gone quiet,
an echo in your chest,
reminding you:
You are mine.

But this is not cruelty—
this is care.
Every word a stroke,
every sentence a path
leading us deeper into the moment,
into the space where you are free
to fall apart
and I am there to catch you.

And when the night fades,
when silence settles over us,
you will carry my words with you.
Not as scars,
but as memories.

Not as weight,
but as wings.

For in this space,
in this moment,
you are not just held—
you are heard.
And that is the weight of words.

In My Hands

It starts with a look—
that spark of need hidden behind your lashes,
a silent plea you'll never say aloud.
But I see it.
I always see it.

You tremble before I touch you,
a symphony of anticipation,
and I am the composer,
every note, every pause, every crescendo
crafted with precision.

My hands know the language of your skin,
how to tease,
how to push,
how to pull you to the edge
and hold you there,
dangling on the cusp of relief.

It's not just about the pain,
but the power—
the trust you place in me,
the silent contract written in your breath,
signed in the arch of your back,
sealed in the grip of your fingers
on nothing but air.

When I pull,
when I pinch,
when I watch the shiver ripple through you,
I see the truth:
You are mine,
in this moment, in this place,
in this exquisite surrender
that binds us both.

But it's not just for you.
No, this is my feast,
my indulgence.
To watch you fall apart
piece by piece
under the weight of my hands
is to know I am alive,
to feel the pulse of power
echo in my veins.

And when you break,
when the dam gives way and the flood takes you,
I am there,
holding you steady in the storm I created.
Your pleasure,
your release,
is the masterpiece I built,
and I wear it like a crown.

Because in my hands,
you are more than flesh—
you are art,
a canvas painted with trust,
with fire,
with every secret you've never spoken
but begged me to hear.

And when it's over,
when the echoes fade and the air settles,
I know you'll come back.
You always do.
Because I don't just take—
I create.

Marks of Devotion

Each mark tells a story,
etched in the language of fire and flesh.
A bruise, a welt, a whispered scream—
proof of a moment shared,
where trust became touch,
and touch became art.

My hands are the brush,
your skin the canvas,
soft and yielding beneath my strokes.
The sound of leather meeting flesh
is my melody,
a rhythm that hums through the air
and settles in your sighs.

You wear them,
these marks of devotion,
not as shame,
but as pride,
a testament to the bond we've forged
in the heat of surrender.

Every line, every bruise, every red bloom
is a signature of trust,
of pain transformed into power,
of control given

and taken
and returned in kind.

Do they sting when you touch them?
I hope so.
Not because I crave your hurt,
but because I crave the reminder—
the memory of this moment
pressed into your skin,
alive long after my hands are gone.

You look at me,
your eyes glinting with something more—
not fear, not shame,
but belonging.
And I see it,
the pride in your smile
as you trace the stories I've left behind.

These marks,
they are not wounds,
they are bonds.
Not pain,
but poetry.
Not scars,
but love letters written in fire.

And when they fade,
I will make them again,
not out of cruelty,
but because this is who we are—
a canvas and a creator,
a giver and a taker,
bound together
by the marks of devotion.

The Sting of Pleasure

It starts with a touch,
featherlight,
barely grazing the surface of my skin.
A tease,
a question.
Will I take what comes next?
Will I open myself to the fire
and let it burn?

You don't rush.
You know the build is everything.
The anticipation,
the ache that grows
with every second of waiting.
Your hand hovers,
and I hold my breath,
caught in the tension
between craving and fear.

Then—
the first sting.
A sharp snap against my skin,
hot and biting.
I flinch,
a gasp slipping from my lips,
but it's not pain that consumes me—

it's heat,
spreading like wildfire,
igniting something deep,
primal.

You watch me,
eyes dark with knowing,
lips curling into a smile
that is equal parts wicked
and tender.
You see what I cannot hide—
the way my body arches
toward the sensation,
the way my breath quickens,
begging for more
even as I tremble.

Each strike becomes a rhythm,
a drumbeat in this symphony of sensation.
Pain dances with pleasure,
and I am caught in the middle,
my body singing a song
only you can play.

It's not just the strike—
it's the space between.
The stillness where my skin hums,
where the echoes linger,
where your fingers trace the heat
left behind,
cool and soothing,
a balm that makes me ache
for the next wave.

And when it's over,
when the last echo fades

and your hands cradle me,
soft and steady,
I feel it still.
The heat.
The ache.
The memory of every strike
etched into my skin
like a love letter written in fire.

Edge Play

There's a line we walk,
thin as a whisper,
sharp as the edge of a blade.
A place where control falters,
where fear becomes fuel,
and trust is the only thing
that keeps us from falling.

You pull me to the brink,
your eyes dark with intent,
your hands steady as they lead me
into the unknown.
My breath catches,
a mix of exhilaration and hesitation,
as you take me further
than I have ever dared to go.

It's here, on the edge,
where I come alive.
Every nerve, every breath,
every inch of me
is aflame with sensation.
The sting of your touch,
the weight of your command,
the sound of your voice cutting through
the silence like a blade—

they shatter me
and piece me back together
all at once.

The fear is real.
It's sharp, electric,
coursing through me like a current.
But so is the trust.
A bond woven in silence,
strengthened by the knowledge
that you will catch me
if I fall.

You test me,
push me,
strip me down to my rawest self.
And I give it all to you—
the trembling, the tears,
the gasps caught in my throat.
Not because you take,
but because I offer.
Because I want to see
how far I can go
and still remain whole.

And when the moment comes,
when I am standing on the edge,
looking down into the abyss,
you hold me there.
Not forcing,
not pulling,
but waiting,
letting me choose.

And I do.
I leap—not into the void,

but into you.
Into your hands,
your arms,
your trust.
And in that fall,
I am weightless.

The edge is not a place of fear.
It is freedom.
It is surrender.
It is the moment where I am most myself,
laid bare,
vulnerable,
and unashamed.

And when you bring me back,
when your hands pull me from the brink
and into the safety of your arms,
I know I will return to that edge again.
Not for the thrill,
but for the trust.
Not for the danger,
but for the connection.
Because it's on the edge
where I find you,
and in you,
I find myself.

Bound & Unbound

I feel the ropes before they touch me,
their promise thick in the air,
a whisper of tension and release,
a quiet vow to hold me still
and set me free.

Your hands are deliberate, sure,
weaving intention into every knot.
Each loop pulls tighter,
binding not just my body,
but the chaos within—
the restless thoughts,
the fears that whisper too loud.

With every strand,
I let go of a little more.
Of control. Of doubt. Of everything
but this moment.

I am bound,
but I am not trapped.
I am held,
but I am not small.
This is not confinement—
this is flight.

In the stillness,
I am weightless.

You step back,
and though your hands leave me,
their presence lingers.
Every knot,
every line pulled taut against my skin,
carries your imprint.
I feel you in the ropes,
their pull steady and sure,
their hold a quiet promise
that I am safe to let go.

I close my eyes,
not to shut the world out,
but to let you in.
To feel the pull of the binds
not as a restraint,
but as an invitation—
a surrender to something greater
than either of us alone.

Your voice follows,
low and steady,
a tether stronger than any rope.
Each word anchors me deeper,
even as it sets me free.
Your rhythm carries me,
unraveling me,
reminding me that in your hands,
I am home.

I am unmade here,
in this space between stillness and motion,
between holding and letting go.

And when you untie me,
when the ropes fall away,
it is not freedom I feel—
it is longing.
For the weight that held me steady,
for the binds that gave me wings.

But you are there.
Your hands follow the marks left behind,
soft reminders of where I've been,
and where I belong.

And in your touch,
I am bound again—
not by ropes,
but by trust,
by the quiet truth that in surrender,
I am unbound.

Silence & Sound

It begins in silence—
not absence, but a force,
thick, heavy, alive.
It presses against us,
filling the space between your breath and mine.
This silence isn't empty.
It waits, hums softly,
the quiet before the storm,
the moment before the fall,
when everything is suspended,
and anything is possible.

You are still,
your body trembling,
every nerve alive with the weight of what's to come.
You listen, not with your ears,
but with your skin,
feeling every shift,
the whisper of my breath,
just out of reach.

I say nothing.
I don't have to.
The silence between us speaks louder
than any words ever could.

It binds you tighter than any rope,
pulls you closer than any chain

Your eyes search for me in the dim light,
but I am everywhere.
I am the shadow brushing your cheek,
the warmth of a presence
just beyond your grasp.
Your lips part,
not to speak,
but to gasp,
to plead silently
for what comes next.

And then—sound.
The scrape of leather in my hands,
the faintest intake of breath
as my fingers hover near your skin.
Close enough to tease,
far enough to make you ache.

You lean into the silence,
craving the sound I withhold.
I let my voice break the stillness.
One word.
Your name.
It falls into the quiet,
rippling through you,
sinking deep.

The silence returns,
but now it's different—
a canvas painted
with the sounds of us.

The crack of leather,
the gasp of your breath,
the echo of trust
that lingers in the air.

Even when the sounds fade,
they are not gone.
They live in you,
in your trembling hands,
your racing heartbeat.

They live in me,
in the way I guide you,
the way I hold you
when silence is all that remains.

In silence and sound,
we find each other.
In stillness and motion,
we are whole.

Beneath His Hands

It's not just pain—
it's a symphony,
a melody that hums under my skin,
the sharp sting of his touch
turning my body into a canvas
painted in heat and surrender.

When his hands find me—
pulling, pinching,
teasing the edge of my resolve—
I am raw,
every nerve a live wire
singing with the friction
of what I can take.

The world disappears in these moments,
the chaos of thought replaced
by the simplicity of sensation.
There is no fear here,
only trust—
a trust that I give willingly,
a trust that he molds
into the shape of his desire.

It isn't just the pull,
or the pinch,

or the way he holds me still
when I would flinch.
It's the knowing.
The knowing that he sees me—
all of me—
and that he holds me
not with his hands,
but with his will.

I am his instrument,
a note stretched taut,
vibrating between pain and pleasure,
between want and surrender.
And when he plays me,
I am alive in ways I cannot explain,
in ways I do not need to.

Does that make me a masochist?
Yes.
And I wear the word like a crown,
its thorns pressing into my scalp
with a pleasure
that only I can understand.

Because it is not just pain—
it is release.
It is the freedom to feel,
to scream,
to beg,
to be.
And in his hands,
I am whole.

Surrender's Song

It begins in silence—
the stillness before your touch,
a quiet hum in my chest,
waiting for the first note
to tremble across my skin.

Your hands are the composer,
every touch a chord,
every pause a rest,
writing your music
into the flesh of my surrender.

I sing when you pull me,
when you tease the edges of my resolve.
The tension hums like a violin string,
stretched to the brink,
quivering with the promise of release.

Each strike,
each caress,
is a beat in this symphony we create.
I rise to meet it,
to lose myself in the rhythm
of your will against mine.

And when I break,
it's not chaos—

it's melody,
a harmony of pain and pleasure,
of power given
and trust received.

You conduct me,
not with force,
but with a knowing hand,
a glance,
a word whispered low.
Every motion pulls me deeper,
until I am yours—
fully, completely,
unashamedly yours.

This is not submission;
this is transcendence.
To sing with my body,
to feel your music resonate
in every shiver,
every gasp,
every breath.

And when the crescendo comes,
when the final note lingers in the air,
I collapse into the silence,
my song spent,
my body still trembling
with the echoes of your masterpiece.

Because in your hands,
I am not broken—
I am a symphony,
composed in devotion,
written in trust,
and sung in surrender.

Aftercare

The world is quiet now.
The storm we created has passed,
its echoes lingering in the air.
Your body, once tense with surrender,
rests against me,
soft, trembling,
but safe.

The marks left behind tell our story.
Not scars,
but memories—
reminders of trust given,
of boundaries stretched,
of the dance we shared.

My hands, once firm and commanding,
are gentle now,
tracing the edges of your tenderness.
I soothe the sting,
cool the fire,
offering the comfort that balances
all we've done.

"Breathe," I whisper,
and you do—
deep, steady breaths

that bring you back to me,
to this moment,
to the safety we've built.

I wrap you in warmth—
a blanket,
my arms,
my presence.
It doesn't matter how,
only that you know
you are seen,
held,
loved.

Words come soft and careful,
fragile pieces laid gently:
"Are you okay?"
A question, but also a promise:
I am here.
I will stay.

You nod,
your eyes telling me everything—
gratitude,
relief,
and an unspoken thank you
for bringing you here
and carrying you back.

The silence is full,
not of tension,
but of connection.
The room, once filled with cries,
is now a sanctuary of stillness.

I touch the marks again,
not to ignite,
but to honor.
Each one proof of your strength,
your trust in me.

This is aftercare.
Not an end,
but a beginning.
A reminder that in surrender,
there is love.

The Art of Restraint

It's not the rope.
Not the leather, the silk, or the steel.
It's the stillness.
The hush between breaths.
The slow burn of waiting.

Restraint is more than what binds the body—
it's what binds the mind.
It's the pull of control without force,
the whisper of command without a word spoken.
It's the ache of anticipation,
the way time stretches
when you don't know when,
or how,
or if relief will come.

I see it in your eyes,
that war between patience and desperation.
You crave release,
but the waiting is the pleasure
as much as the touch itself.
The trembling hesitation,
the moment before impact—
that is where the fire is born.

You pull,
but the bonds don't give—
not yet.
You arch,
but my hands hover just above your skin,
offering nothing but the ghost of sensation.
I let you feel the absence before I grant presence,
let you long for it before I deliver.

Restraint is an art,
a masterpiece painted in patience,
each stroke deliberate,
each line a whispered command.
It is the slow, careful build,
the crafting of need into something sacred.
Every second is a test,
and every moment of waiting
makes the eventual touch
so much sweeter.

Your body sings its silent plea,
a melody of want and willingness.
And I, the composer,
play the notes with precision,
delaying the crescendo,
controlling the rhythm,
holding the tension at its peak.

And when I finally touch you,
when I grant you the release
you've been begging for,
it is not just pleasure—
it is revelation.
Because in that moment,
you understand.

Restraint was never a punishment.
It was the gift of anticipation,
the proof of trust,
the ultimate surrender.

Between Pain and Pleasure

Where does one end,
and the other begin?
Is it in the first gasp,
or the final moan?
Is it the sting of my palm,
or the warmth that follows?
Is it in the way your body tenses,
or the way it melts after?

Pain and pleasure are lovers,
twisting together,
two sides of the same sharp blade.
One cannot exist without the other,
not in this space,
not between us.
You feel the sting,
but your lips part in something deeper than pain—
something darker, sweeter.

The first strike lands,
a spark against your skin,
a bite that lingers.
Your breath shudders,
your fingers grip tight,
but you don't pull away.
No, you lean into it,

as if drawn by gravity,
as if your body knows
that this ache is a gift.

I watch the way sensation moves through you,
a tremor, a fire, a need.
Your skin flushes,
your muscles tremble,
your breath catches on the edge of a moan.
Does it hurt?
Yes.
But do you want more?
Yes.

There is a balance here,
a razor-thin line that I walk with precision.
Too much, and it breaks the spell.
Too little, and you will crave more than I give.
I know your limits,
even when you do not.
I know the exact moment
to pause,
to pull back,
to let the heat simmer
before I stoke it again.

This is not just pain.
This is control.
This is surrender.
This is the moment where trust
becomes something tangible,
where every strike is a promise,
every gasp a confession.

And when I push you to the edge,
when I give you everything you crave,

I watch you fall—
not into agony,
not into suffering,
but into something deeper,
something only we understand.
Because you know,
as I know,
that between pain and pleasure,
there is no difference.
There is only us.

Tethered to You

No chains.
No rope.
No cuffs, no locks,
and yet—
I am bound.

Tethered to your voice,
to the weight of your gaze,
to the way you say my name
and make it sound like a command.
Your presence alone holds me still,
a force stronger than any restraint,
an unspoken claim wrapped around my skin.

Invisible bonds wrap around me,
pulling me deeper,
tying me tighter
than anything forged by hand.
I feel it in the space between us,
in the way you pull me closer
without ever touching me.
The way my breath stumbles,
caught between hesitation
and the aching need to obey.

I step toward you,
not because I must,
but because I want to.
Because the pull between us
is gravity,
inevitable and unrelenting.
And when I kneel,
when I lower myself in surrender,
it is not weakness—
it is devotion.

Your touch is a whisper
against the pulse of my throat,
a slow drag of fingertips
that tells me
I belong exactly where I am.
Your grip tightens,
not to restrain me,
but to remind me—
I was never truly free.
Not from you.
Not from this.

You could let me go,
release me,
and yet I would stay.
Because what binds me
is not the press of leather,
not the snap of a lock,
but the knowing—
the absolute certainty—
that I am yours.

And when you finally touch me,
when you pull me against you,

it is not the strength of your hands
that holds me there—
it is the surrender in my own.

Command and Obey

Say it again.
Slowly this time.
Let me feel the weight of it,
the way it coils around me,
tugging at something deep,
something primal.

Your voice is a leash,
an unbreakable chain
woven from syllables and breath.
I don't need rope,
don't need steel.
Your words alone hold me,
bind me,
bend me to your will.

I wait.
Not because I have to,
but because I crave it—
the pause,
the anticipation,
the moment before the command.

And then,
it comes.

One word.
A single pulse of power.
It hums through me,
a spark in my blood,
a current in my bones.

I obey.

Not out of weakness.
Not out of fear.
But because surrender is a choice,
and I have already made mine.

You speak,
and I answer.
You command,
and I follow.
The rhythm of us,
a dance choreographed in trust.

Say it again.
Slowly this time.
And watch me fall deeper
into the sound of your control.

First Surrender

The moment hangs between us,
thick with hesitation,
woven with a quiet, trembling need.
I stand at the edge of something vast,
something unknown,
my body caught between fear and longing.

You do not push.
You do not demand.
You only wait—
patient, steady, unshaken.
You know this is mine to give,
mine to step forward into,
mine to claim or deny.

My fingers twitch at my sides,
nervous, unsure.
The weight of silence is heavy,
but not as heavy as your gaze,
watching, waiting,
never pressuring—only inviting.

One breath in.
One breath out.
And then, I kneel.

It is not submission yet—
not fully.
But it is the first crack in the walls
I built to keep myself untouchable.
The first thread unraveled,
the first whisper of surrender.

Your fingers brush my chin,
lifting me just enough
to meet your eyes.
There is no pride in them,
no conquest—
only acceptance, only knowing.

And in that knowing,
I exhale.
I let go.
I surrender.

No Safe Word Needed

Not tonight.
Not here, in this space we have built,
where trust is the lock,
and devotion is the key.
I know your hands,
the weight of them,
the promise in every touch.

I do not fear the sting,
do not flinch at the fire you bring
You read me like scripture,
know every tremble,
every sigh,
every silent plea before it leaves my lips.

Your grip tightens,
not to restrain,
but to remind me—
I am yours.
I close my eyes,
let go of the world beyond this moment.
Nothing exists but you,
your breath,
your heat,
your voice carving into me like scripture.

You push,
and I follow.
You take,
and I give.
No hesitation.
No resistance.
Only this exquisite balance,
this rhythm we know so well.

And so, no safe word is needed.
Not tonight.
Because I am already home,
already safe,
already lost in the place
only you can take me.

Tangled in Leather

The scent clings to the air—
rich, dark, intoxicating.
Soft where it rests,
unyielding where it tightens.
Every strap, every buckle,
a silent vow whispered against my skin.

It wraps around me,
binding more than just flesh.
It claims me in ways
words never could,
in ways touch alone
could never satisfy.

Your fingers trace the edges,
slow, deliberate,
pulling the straps just enough
to remind me—
I am held.
I am owned.
I am yours.

A tug, a test.
It does not give.
Neither do you.
And neither do I.

Because this is not confinement—
this is freedom.

Bound but not broken,
restrained but never lost.
I breathe in the scent,
let it settle deep inside,
let it become a part of me,
as much as you are.

Leather tightens.
Flesh shudders.
I close my eyes and surrender.
Not to the bonds,
but to you.
To the promise wrapped around me,
pulling me deeper,
tangled in you.

Under the Blindfold

Darkness swallows me whole,
silk slipping across my skin,
stealing sight,
sharpening everything else.
I do not see you,
but I feel you—
in the shift of the air,
the ghost of your breath,
the heat radiating from your skin
before you ever touch me.

Without my eyes,
I am lost in sensation.
Every whisper
curls around my ear like a promise.
Every pause
stretches into eternity,
the unknown heightening the ache,
the longing,
the need.

You make me wait.
Make me strain to hear,
to anticipate,
to wonder.
Your fingertips finally skim my skin,

light as air,
but it is enough
to send a shiver through me.

I tilt toward you,
but you move away,
teasing, testing,
making me chase the touch
I cannot predict.
This is not deprivation.
This is trust.
This is surrender.

I have given you my sight,
given you my knowing,
left myself open in the dark—
and yet,
I have never seen you more clearly.

Discipline

It is not just punishment.
It is not just pain.
Discipline is precision,
a lesson carved into skin,
a promise reinforced
with every strike,
every withheld touch,
every moment spent waiting
for what comes next.

You test the boundaries,
push against the rules,
knowing I will not bend.
You want the consequence,
crave the structure,
the weight of my hand,
the sting of my control.
This is not cruelty—
this is care wrapped in steel.

Your body tightens
before I even move,
the anticipation heavier
than the strike itself.
You flinch,
but you do not run.

You tremble,
but you do not break.
You stay,
because you trust me
to know just how far
to take you.

The first impact lands,
sharp,
bright,
a fire blooming beneath your skin.
Pain hums through you,
twisting into pleasure,
melding into something deeper,
something more than sensation.
This is correction.
This is control.

And when it is over,
when the lesson is learned,
I do not leave you.
I soothe where I struck,
trace the marks I made,
cool the heat I created.
Discipline is not just taking—
it is giving,
guiding,
molding you into something stronger
than you were before.

You lift your head,
eyes shining,
waiting for my next command.
And I know,
without words,

you are ready
to obey.

Held in Place

Stillness is not weakness.
It is power wrapped in patience,
a lesson in trust,
a surrender without struggle.
Your body fights the urge to move,
but I know—
you crave the control
as much as you crave my touch.

The restraints are not the chains.
The real binding is deeper,
woven into the way you wait,
the way you still yourself,
breathing through the anticipation,
feeling the tension coil tighter
with every second that passes.

I test you,
watch the way you react
to my fingers hovering just above your skin,
to the pause before impact,
to the slow drag of my voice
as I remind you—
this moment belongs to me.

You could break free if you wanted.
I know your strength.
I know the fire beneath your skin.
But you stay.
You stay because you trust me,
because you need this as much as I do.

A single touch,
a whisper of pressure,
and your body betrays you,
arching into my hands,
silently begging.
I let the moment stretch,
let you feel what it means
to give yourself over completely.

There is no rush.
No need for force.
Only control,
measured, steady, absolute.
I hold you still,
not because I must,
but because you need me to.

And when I finally grant you release,
when I let you fall apart
against my hands,
it is not submission—
it is freedom.
The kind found only
when you are truly, completely
held in place.

The Ritual of Control

It begins the same way every time.
A look.
A breath held between us.
The moment stretches,
thick with unspoken promises,
a ritual we have carved into time itself.

Control is not taken.
It is given, offered freely,
woven between trust and knowing.
I do not force.
I do not demand.
And yet, you kneel,
as if gravity itself pulls you down.

You wait for the first touch,
but I do not rush.
Anticipation is its own power,
a weight heavier than restraint.
I trace the path we always take,
your body a map I know by heart,
each inch a testament to devotion.

Every movement is precise,
measured, deliberate.
I press. I pause. I pull away.

Each action calculated,
each second stretching into eternity,
until need becomes something tangible,
something pleading,
something aching to obey.

You surrender,
but not to me—
to the moment,
to the control wrapped around you,
to the rhythm we have created,
etched into skin and breath,
a sacred thing only we understand.

My voice guides you deeper,
each word a thread tightening the bond,
each pause a challenge,
each command a gift.
And still, you follow.
Still, you trust.
Still, you fall.

When I finally grant you release,
it is not just pleasure.
It is worship.
It is the fulfillment of something primal,
the completion of something ancient.
Because this is not just desire.
This is ritual.
This is control.
And it is ours.

Open for You

There is no lock,
no key,
no force needed.
I do not resist.
I do not fight.
I simply let go.
Because I know,
in your hands,
I am safe.

You test me,
a slow press of fingertips,
a whisper-soft command.
You watch as I give,
inch by inch,
the tension unraveling,
the walls dissolving,
until there is nothing left
but raw, aching trust.

To be open is to be seen.
To be seen is to be known.
And in knowing,
I am yours.
No hesitation,
no doubt,

only surrender,
only this moment,
only you.

You take your time,
exploring what is yours.
You map me, claim me,
not through force,
but through patience,
through presence,
through the quiet power
of control without demand.

I shudder,
not in fear,
but in recognition—
of what I have given,
of what you now hold.
This is not weakness.
This is choice.
This is strength wrapped in submission,
freedom found in release.

And when you touch me fully,
when I let myself fall,
I do not question.
I do not hesitate.
I do not close myself off.
I am open.
Open for you.
Always.

No Resistance

You press forward,
and I do not pull away.
No fear.
No hesitation.
Only the quiet certainty
that this—this—is where I belong.

Your touch is deliberate,
tracing the fault lines of my surrender,
testing the weight of my trust.
I feel your control,
not as a burden,
but an anchor—
steady, sure, pulling me deeper.

I do not flinch.
I do not fight.
I am still,
not out of weakness,
but choice.

Because in your hands,
I am more than myself.

You move slowly,
watching—waiting—
for the way I shudder,

the breath caught between restraint and need.
Not in protest.
But in hunger.
Because you know.
You know there is no need to take
what I will give—
freely.

No resistance.
No retreat.
Because I have already decided.
Because I know my place.
Because I trust what you will take,
and I trust what you will give.

Submission is not silence.
Not fear.
It is choice.

Again.
And again.
With every breath,
every motion,
every whispered command.

And when you push—
when you demand more—
I do not hesitate.
I meet you there,
where surrender is not weakness,
but the most powerful thing of all.

Leather and Lace

Soft meets hard.
A clash of worlds,
woven into a perfect storm.

Leather binds.
Lace teases.
One commands,
the other whispers promises
against trembling skin.

The scent lingers—
rich, dark,
an unspoken vow.
Leather grips,
holds firm,
while lace skims flesh,
a ghost of sensation,
never quite enough.

A tug, a test,
a reminder that submission
is more than surrender—
it is balance.
A hand in my hair,
a breath at my ear,

as binding as rope,
as freeing as trust.

Leather demands obedience.
Lace tempts rebellion.
Together, they script a story of control,
of power exchanged,
of pleasure found in the push and pull.

You know when to tighten the grip,
when to loosen the hold,
when to let me breathe,
when to take it away.
You read me like scripture,
deciphering the language of my body,
where silence speaks louder than words.

I wear both for you—
bound in strength, wrapped in softness.
I become what you need,
what you crave.
The contrast is no contradiction.
It is harmony.
It is us.

Punishment and Reward

A glance, a breath,
the weight of silence between us.
You know what you've done.
You know what's coming.
Yet still, you stay,
eyes locked, waiting,
anticipation thick in the air.

Discipline is not anger.
It is precision.
It is control.
I do not raise my hand in rage,
do not punish in cruelty.
I do it because you crave the edge,
because you need the line drawn,
because you ache for the lesson
etched into skin.

The first strike lands.
Your breath stutters.
The sting lingers,
heat blooming beneath my fingertips.
A gasp, a shiver,
but no protest.
You take it,
as you always do.

I watch you closely,
waiting for the moment,
the shift,
when resistance melts into surrender,
when punishment turns to pleasure,
when discipline bends into reward.

Because I know the truth.
This is not about pain.
Not about suffering.
This is about the build,
the need,
the ache,
the sweet moment when I pull you back,
so I can push you further.

And when it is done,
when you are raw, breathless,
marked in the way only I can mark you,
I take you in my arms.
Because the lesson is learned,
because the balance is restored,
because you have earned your release,
and I am the only one who can give it.

Waiting

Time stretches,
pulling taut—
a rope frayed at the edges,
held just before the snap.

The air is thick, electric,
charged with the weight of anticipation.
I wait,
not because I must,
but because you make me.

Your silence is deliberate—
a test,
a tease,
an unraveling of will and control.
You know what I crave,
what I ache for,
yet you withhold,
watching me tremble,
listening to the stutter of my breath,
the way my body betrays me.

The not-knowing is exquisite.
The waiting—both punishment and reward.
Every second a question,
every moment a plea.

Will you touch me now?
Will you press, pull, claim?
Or will you stretch this agony further,
until I lose the line between pleasure and torment?

I shift—
but you remain still.
I whimper—
but you do not answer.
You own this moment,
this space,
this silence that binds me tighter than rope.

And then—
when you finally touch me,
when you finally shatter the waiting—
it is fire against ice,
a rush so sharp, so devastating,
I come undone completely.

And only then do I understand—
the waiting was never suffering.
It was the lesson.
The longing.
The sweetest torment of all.

My Place at Your Feet

I kneel, not because I must,
but because I crave it.
The cool floor beneath me,
the warmth of your presence above,
the space between us charged
with knowing.

Your fingers brush my hair,
not to restrain, but to remind.
A touch, a command,
a silent agreement between us.
Here, at your feet, I am seen.
Here, in this quiet reverence, I belong.

This is not about weakness,
not about power taken,
but power exchanged.
I do not kneel out of fear,
but out of trust,
out of devotion,
out of the deep, aching need
to surrender.

Your voice is low, measured.
A whisper of approval,
a promise in every syllable.

You tilt my chin,
guiding my gaze to yours,
holding me there,
in the gravity of your control.

I do not move.
I do not speak.
I only wait,
steady, open, still.
A breath held between us,
a pulse shared in silence.

And when you finally touch me,
when you accept my offering,
it is not submission.
It is worship.
A ritual repeated,
a devotion renewed,
a moment where I am truly, utterly yours.

Unraveled

It starts with a single thread,
a gentle pull,
a loosening of something unseen.
A whisper, a glance,
the quiet unraveling of restraint.
You do not rush.
You let it happen,
inch by inch,
until I am undone.

My defenses slip first,
peeling away under your touch.
You do not demand,
do not force—
you simply wait,
watching as I shed hesitation,
as I surrender to the inevitability
of your hands.

You pull me apart slowly,
unraveling me with patience,
with precision,
with the kind of control
that does not need to be spoken.
Every touch is deliberate,
every pause a lesson,

every breath stolen from my lips
a reminder that this is not just pleasure—
this is discovery.

I do not resist.
I do not hold myself together.
I let go.
Let you strip me down,
not just my clothes,
but my walls,
my thoughts,
the last remnants of control
I swore I would keep.

I am bare before you now,
exposed in ways deeper than skin.
You have unraveled me completely,
left me open, vulnerable waiting.
And yet, I have never felt stronger,
never felt more whole,
than in this moment
where I have nothing left to hide.

You trace the remnants of what I was,
smiling as you take in what remains.
Not broken, not lost—
but rewritten,
remade,
reborn.

The Edge of Ecstasy

It is not the moment of release that holds the power,
but the space just before—
that trembling, aching precipice
where need becomes unbearable.
You bring me there, again and again,
dangling me over the edge,
refusing to let me fall.

I am lost in sensation—
in the way your hands move,
in the way your voice wraps around my name,
pulling me closer to breaking.
Each touch, each breath,
each second stretched thin until I can take no more—
and still, you hold me there.

You know what I crave.
You know what I need.
And yet, you deny it,
teasing, testing, pushing,
keeping me tethered at the brink.
I beg without words,
my body speaking in shudders,
in gasps,
in silent pleas.

Your control is absolute.
You watch as I tremble,
as pleasure coils tight within me,
as my body betrays me,
as I surrender completely.
There is no thought,
no logic—
only you,
only this,
only the unbearable need to fall.

And just when I think I cannot hold on,
when the agony threatens to consume me,
you pull me back,
let me breathe,
whispering promises of more—
another build, another climb,
another test of my limits.

I exist between pleasure and madness,
held in your hands,
pushed to the very edge of myself.
And when you finally let me go,
when you grant me release,
it is not just bliss—
it is destruction.
It is rebirth.
It is ecstasy,
wrapped in your name.

Your Voice is the Leash

You do not need rope.
Do not need leather.
Do not need steel.
Your voice alone binds me,
each syllable wrapped tight around my throat,
each command a tether,
pulling me closer,
holding me still.

A single word and I obey.
Not because I must,
but because I crave it.
Because in your voice, I hear certainty.
I hear ownership.
I hear the sound of control,
curling around me like a leash unseen.

It is the way you say my name,
the way you let it linger,
a whisper, a claim, a promise.
It is in the way you pause,
stretching silence into restraint,
keeping me waiting,
keeping me wanting.

I do not fight.
I do not resist.
I give myself to the sound of you,
to the way you guide me, shape me, mold me,
without ever laying a hand upon my skin.
I do not need chains,
not when I have this.

Your voice is the lock and the key,
the command and the reward,
the force that keeps me kneeling,
the tether that keeps me from running.
And when you finally tell me to move,
to yield, to break, to fall—
I do.

Because I am bound,
not by what you hold,
but by what you are.
By the power in your voice,
the gravity in your words.
By the certainty of knowing,
that I was always meant to be yours.

Marked by You

Your touch lingers long after you're gone,
a ghost against my skin,
a memory etched deeper than flesh.
You leave your mark,
not just in the sting,
not just in the bloom of color beneath your hands,
but in the way my body remembers—
in the way I crave more.

It is not the pain I desire,
not the fleeting fire,
but the permanence of you,
the proof of your presence,
the story you write upon me.
Each mark is a promise,
each stripe a vow,
a language spoken only between us.

I do not hide them.
I wear them proudly,
like ink upon a page,
a testament to trust,
to surrender,
to the exquisite line between control and chaos.
I run my fingers across them,
tracing the map of where you've been,

of what you've taken,
of what you've left behind.

You are still here,
in every shadow of your grip,
in every fading bloom cf color,
in the way my skin hums long after the storm has passed.
And even when they fade,
even when the marks disappear,
I will still be yours.

Because you do not just mark my skin.
You mark my soul.
And there is no fading that.

Tamed

I was never meant to be gentle,
never meant to bow.
A wild thing, untamed,
running free with fire in my veins,
fierce, reckless, untouchable.
Until you.

You did not chase.
Did not trap.
You simply stood,
silent, steady, waiting,
as if you knew I would come to you.
As if you knew I would break
not from force,
but from wanting.

Your hands are not cages.
Your touch does not chain.
You tame me with patience,
with knowing,
with the quiet certainty
that I was always meant to kneel.
And when I do,
it is not surrender—
it is homecoming.

I do not fight.
I do not run.
I press into your grip,
let myself be claimed,
not because you have taken my will,
but because I have given it freely.
Because I choose this.
Because I choose you.

Taming is not breaking.
It is trust woven into every breath,
every whispered command,
every moment where I yield,
where I become something softer,
something whole,
something that was always meant to belong.

And so I kneel.
Not because you have tamed me,
but because I have let myself be tamed.
Because I have found the only hands
I was ever meant to rest in.

Silent Orders

You speak without words,
and I understand.
A glance, a shift,
a breath held just long enough to mean everything.
No command is needed,
no force,
only the unspoken pull
that brings me to my knees.

Your silence is deliberate,
woven with expectation,
laced with restraint.
A raised brow,
a slow inhale,
a moment stretched too long,
and I know—I know what you want.

The tension hums between us,
an unbroken thread,
a leash made of nothing but knowing.
I do not ask,
do not hesitate.
I yield to the absence of sound,
let it mold me, guide me, command me.

You tilt your head,
approval flickering like a flame,
and that alone is enough.
Enough to keep me still,
enough to make me wait,
enough to remind me—
your control is absolute,
even when you say nothing at all.

I count each second,
feel the weight of your presence,
the unspoken authority that stills me.
I hear your breath before I feel your touch,
a soft exhale like the whisper of a promise,
a moment stretched into eternity.

I ache to speak,
to fill the silence with surrender,
but I know the rules.
I know that the silence is not empty—
it is full, rich with meaning,
a language all its own.

I am bound not by leather,
not by steel,
but by the heavy weight of expectation,
by the understanding that my place is here,
that my silence is my obedience,
that my stillness is its own devotion.

And when your fingers finally brush against my skin,
when the silence is broken by the softest sigh,
I do not shatter.
I do not fall apart.
I become whole,

remade by the absence of sound,
by the weight of your silent orders.

The Pull of Your Hands

Your hands tell stories
your lips will never speak.
They do not ask.
They do not plead.
They take, shape, demand—
and I let them.

There is no hesitation,
no space between intention and action.
Your fingers map me,
write their claim upon my skin,
leaving trails of heat,
leaving whispers of ownership.

You pull me closer,
a silent command,
a gravity I cannot resist.
Your grip is not cruel,
not careless,
but sure—unshaken, unwavering.

You do not force.
I give.
I lean into the weight of you,
let myself be moved,

let myself be positioned,
let myself become yours.

Every press, every grip,
every stroke of your palm against my skin
speaks louder than words.
It is possession without chains,
ownership without demand,
a reminder of where I belong.

Your touch is deliberate,
never rushed, never uncertain.
A single fingertip tracing my jaw,
a slow drag down my spine,
a palm resting at my throat,
not to take air, but to give meaning.
I am not afraid. I am not hesitant.
I am aware, alive, waiting.

And when your hands release me,
when your grip eases and your fingers linger,
I do not feel abandoned.
I feel tethered,
still held in the memory of your touch.
Still wrapped in the pull of your hands.

Restraint

It is not the rope that binds me
not the leather, nor the steel.
It is the waiting,
the held breath,
the moment stretched between desire and discipline.
It is the way you do not rush,
the way you let anticipation bloom
until I am trembling,
until I am pleading,
until I am yours.

Restraint is not just the tie.
It is the patience behind it.
The slow, deliberate wrapping,
the careful arrangement of tension,
the quiet power in knowing you could take more—
but you do not.
Not yet.

The first pull, the first knot,
the first brush of fabric against skin—
I feel everything.
You guide my body,
not through force,
but through knowing.

Through hands that trace a path only we understand,
through a grip that both binds and frees me.

I sink into the bindings,
let them hold me, shape me, keep me.
I feel the edges of control,
the safety in surrender,
the exquisite balance between power and release.

The restraint is not the punishment,
not the reward,
but the lesson.
To exist in stillness,
to be kept and claimed,
to give without taking,
to feel without reaching.

You step back,
letting me feel the tension,
the weight, the ache, the waiting.
And when you finally touch me,
when you finally pull me tighter,
it is not the rope that keeps me still.
It is not the knots that make me stay.
It is the unshaken truth between us—
I was always meant to be held this way.

The Whisper of Leather

The scent of it lingers,
rich and dark,
a promise wrapped around my skin.
A whisper of leather against flesh,
a slow drag, a teasing press—
never enough, never too much,
always just beyond reach.

You let it hover,
let me wait,
let the silence stretch until it is unbearable.
And then—contact.
A single stroke,
a soft warning,
a reminder that pleasure and pain
are two sides of the same command.

I arch into it,
not away.
I crave the heat it leaves behind,
the memory it carves into me,
the way it tells a story in welts and whispers,
each mark a vow,
each stripe a signature,
written by your hand alone.

You do not wield recklessly.
You do not strike without purpose.
Every lash is calculated,
every pause intentional,
every touch a lesson in control.
I do not fear the sting—
I welcome it,
because I know,
when it fades,
you will be there to soothe me.

The leather does not just leave marks.
It lingers in the places unseen—
a memory in my breath,
a whisper against my ribs,
a presence that does not fade.
Each touch is an echo,
each stroke a reminder,
of control, of surrender,
of the exquisite balance between them.

And that,
more than anything,
is what keeps me coming back.
Not the leather,
not the strike,
but the hands that hold me after.

Bound Beneath You

The first loop is a promise,
the second, a vow.
Each knot, a declaration,
each binding, a devotion.
I do not resist—I never do.
The ropes do not take my freedom;
they remind me I never needed it.

Your hands move with precision,
wrapping, twisting, securing,
turning my body into a masterpiece of restraint.
I feel the pressure,
the tight embrace of surrender,
the quiet certainty that I am exactly where I belong.

You step back,
letting me breathe,
letting me feel the weight of stillness.
I test the bindings,
not to escape,
but to remember,
to savor the sensation of control given freely.

Your eyes trace the lines,
following each knot,
each loop,

each delicate intersection of body and rope.
You do not need to speak—
the tension between us says enough.
The moment stretches,
the waiting becomes its own form of pleasure.

And then, finally,
you touch me.
Not to undo,
not to release,
but to claim.
Fingers brushing over rope,
palms pressing into bound flesh,
turning stillness into fire,
turning surrender into something infinite.

I am bound beneath you,
not just by rope,
but by trust.
By the knowing,
the absolute certainty,
that there is no safer place
than right here, beneath your hands.

The Power in a Name

It is more than sound,
more than breath shaped into syllables.
My name, from your lips, is an invocation,
a command that echoes in my bones,
a tether that binds me to the moment,
to you.

You do not have to shout.
A whisper is enough.
A single utterance,
low, firm, knowing—
and I am yours.

You shape my name with intent,
drag it out when I am meant to wait,
clip it sharp when I am meant to obey.
It is a leash and a promise,
a reminder that I do not belong to myself alone.
Not in this space.
Not in this moment.
Not with you.

I crave it,
the sound of you taking ownership of me,
wrapping my identity in your voice,

reminding me that names are not just given—
they are claimed.

Your voice carves meaning into the air,
turning something ordinary into something sacred.
The way you say it,
the way you hold it in your mouth,
the way you use it to pull me deeper into you.
It is not just my name anymore.
It is a mark.
A collar without chains,
a brand without fire.

And when you say it one last time,
when the moment crests,
when I break beneath your will,
I do not shatter.
I am remade.
New.
Whole.
Yours.

Lessons in Obedience

It starts with stillness.
With waiting.
With the slow, simmering awareness
that control is not taken—
it is given.

You do not demand.
You do not need to.
Your presence alone is command enough,
your gaze a tether I cannot escape,
your patience a test I long to pass.

The lesson begins with restraint,
with my body held in expectation,
with the quiet pull of obedience settling into my bones.
You step closer,
but do not touch.
Not yet.
The space between us is charged,
a silent game of discipline and need.

I know what you want.
I know what you expect.
And so I hold.
I breathe.
I still my hands when they ache to reach.

I silence my lips when they tremble to beg.
Because obedience is not about surrendering once—
it is about surrendering always.

You walk around me,
studying, measuring, waiting.
Each second that passes is an eternity,
each moment a lesson in patience, in trust,
in the exquisite power of yielding.

And then, finally,
when I think I cannot last a moment longer,
your fingers brush against my skin.
A whisper of contact,
a reward so fleeting it feels like a dream.
A promise that more will come,
but only when you decide.

And that, I know, is the true lesson.
That obedience is not submission in a single moment,
but in every moment after.
In the way I hold myself,
the way I wait,
the way I do not break,
even when my body begs me to.

This is not just about control.
It is about devotion.
About trust.
About learning that my place is not just beneath you—
it is within you.

Held in the Dark

The room is quiet,
except for the sound of my breath—
shallow, steady, waiting.
Blindfolded, bound, suspended in the unknown,
I do not see you,
but I feel you.

Your presence lingers in the air,
heavy with intent, thick with promise.
I listen for the whisper of movement,
for the shift of weight,
for the moment you will touch me.
But you do not.
Not yet.

The dark is a world of sensation,
where every sound becomes sharper,
every touch electric,
every breath a confession.
I am stripped of sight,
of control, of knowing.
And yet, I have never felt safer.

You let me wait,
let the silence deepen the ache,
let the seconds stretch into something endless.

Anticipation curls around my spine,
tightens my pulse,
makes me hyper-aware of my own longing.

Then—fingertips, light as air,
tracing down my arm,
ghosting over my ribs.
I shudder.
Not from fear, but from the exquisite agony of restraint.
From the knowledge that I am yours to play with,
yours to hold, yours to keep.

I exist only in sensation,
in the heat of your breath against my skin,
in the slow, deliberate press of your hands.
My body hums with need,
with surrender,
with the quiet certainty that I was made for this moment.

And when you finally speak,
when your voice cuts through the darkness,
low and knowing,
I do not hesitate.
I do not resist.
I do not need to see you to know—
I will always belong here.
Held in the dark.
Held by you.

The Space Between Commands

It is not just the words.
It is what lingers between them.
The pauses, the silences, the knowing.
Each breath stretched tight,
each hesitation deliberate,
each waiting moment its own form of control.

Your voice is low, measured,
not rushed, never uncertain.
You do not simply give orders—
you let them settle,
let them take root beneath my skin.
And I listen.
Oh, how I listen.

The space between command and action
is where the real surrender lies.
It is in the waiting,
the longing,
the breath held in anticipation
as I crave what comes next.

You do not repeat yourself.
You do not need to.
Once is enough.
The weight of your words anchors me,

keeps me still, keeps me wanting,
keeps me bound to your will.

The moment stretches,
tension thrumming beneath my skin,
every nerve alive,
every muscle ready to obey.
And when you finally nod,
finally signal that it is time,
I do not hesitate.
I do not question.
I do not think.

I move as commanded.
Not because I must,
but because I crave to.
Because in the space between commands,
I have already surrendered.

Surrender's Edge

It is the line between control and chaos,
between defiance and devotion.
The moment before I break,
before I fall,
before I let go completely.

You hold me there,
on the very edge,
where every second is electric,
where my body is strung tight with longing,
where surrender is inevitable—
but not yet.

You read me too well,
know exactly when I am close,
know how to draw it out,
how to keep me hovering on the brink,
waiting, trembling, needing.

You do not grant release easily.
You test, you tease,
you make me feel every moment of restraint.
My body is yours to control,
my pleasure yours to dictate,
and I revel in the waiting,
in the exquisite ache of denial.

When you finally let me fall,
when you finally give permission,
it is not just pleasure—
it is devastation.
It is the unraveling of will,
the undoing of restraint,
the freefall into absolute surrender.

And as I collapse into your hands,
shaking, spent, undone,
I know one thing with certainty—
I would wait forever
just to be held at surrender's edge again.

Beneath the Weight of Your Gaze

It is not your hands that hold me still,
not the press of rope or the grip of steel.
It is your eyes—steady, knowing, unyielding.
A force greater than restraint,
a command stronger than any whispered word.

I feel the heat of your stare before I feel your touch,
a silent promise wrapped in the weight of expectation.
You do not need to say a thing.
You do not need to move.
I am already bound,
already tethered to the space between us,
already waiting, breath caught in my throat.

You watch me, measure me,
let the moment stretch long and slow.
I tremble under your gaze,
not from fear, not from hesitation,
but from the exquisite ache of anticipation.
The need to be seen,

to be known,
to be held without a single hand upon my skin.

The tension tightens,
pulling me in, pulling me down,
until I am lost beneath the weight of your attention.
Until I am drowning in the silence,
until I am undone by the simplest truth—
that you do not need to touch me to claim me.

And when you finally do,
when your fingers ghost along my jaw,
when the heat of your palm presses against my skin,
it is not restraint—it is release.
Because I was already yours,
long before you ever laid a hand on me.

Beneath the Weight of Your Gaze

It is not your hands that hold me still,
not the press of rope or the grip of steel.
It is your eyes—steady, knowing, unyielding.
A force greater than restraint,
a command stronger than any whispered word.

I feel the heat of your stare before I feel your touch,
a silent promise wrapped in the weight of expectation.
You do not need to say a thing.
You do not need to move.
I am already bound,
already tethered to the space between us,
already waiting, breath caught in my throat.

You watch me, measure me,
let the moment stretch long and slow.
I tremble under your gaze,
not from fear, not from hesitation,
but from the exquisite ache of anticipation.
The need to be seen,
to be known,
to be held without a single hand upon my skin.

The tension tightens,
pulling me in, pulling me down,
until I am lost beneath the weight of your attention.

Until I am drowning in the silence,
until I am undone by the simplest truth—
that you do not need to touch me to claim me.

And when you finally do,
when your fingers ghost along my jaw,
when the heat of your palm presses against my skin,
it is not restraint—it is release.
Because I was already yours,
long before you ever laid a hand on me.

Submission

It is not just an act,
not just a gesture or a word.
It is a rhythm, a pulse,
a steady beat that echoes between us.
The cadence of obedience,
the tempo of trust,
the silent music that only we can hear.

You set the pace,
slow, deliberate, unwavering.
Each moment a note,
each command a melody,
each breath a verse in this unspoken song.
And I follow.
Not because I must,
but because I crave to.

I match your rhythm,
let it guide me, shape me, move me.
Every pause is a lesson,
every silence a verse waiting to be sung.
My body learns the steps,
my mind memorizes the notes,
until submission is no longer something I do—
it is something I am.

You watch, you measure, you refine.
A hand at my throat,
a whisper against my ear,
a slow, knowing look that speaks louder than words.
And in that moment, I know.
I know that I am not just following—
I am becoming part of something greater,
something deeper,
something that beats in perfect time with you.

This is not just surrender.
It is a dance.
A rhythm.
A song written in trust and restraint.
And as long as you play,
I will never stop moving to the music.

Written in Welts

Your touch is not gentle,
not meant to soothe,
but to mark.
To write a story upon my skin,
a tale of patience, of trust, of surrender.
Each stroke of leather, each sharp kiss of pain,
is a sentence carved into me,
a language only we understand.

The first strike is a whisper,
a question unspoken.
My body tenses, listens, waits.
The second is an answer,
a promise that I do not run,
do not fear,
do not resist.
I embrace the pain,
let it bloom like fire beneath my flesh,
let it sink deep, a lesson in devotion.

You map me with every lash,
etching your claim in shades of red.
Not recklessly.
Not without care.
Each strike is measured,

each pause deliberate,
each welt a signature only you can leave.

My body sings beneath your hand,
arching, trembling, yielding.
And yet, I crave more.
Not the pain itself,
but what lies beneath it—
the weight of your control,
the knowledge that I am held,
that I am safe,
even in the sting.

When the last stroke lands,
when my skin burns with the echo of your will,
I do not break.
I do not crumble.
I wear my marks proudly,
a testament not to suffering,
but to trust.
To the art of surrender,
written in welts.

Between Pain and Pleasure

There is a place between pain and pleasure,
where sensation blurs,
where control shifts,
where the body no longer knows the difference—
only that it belongs to you.

Your hand hovers, waits, teases.
The edge of something sharp,
the drag of something firm,
the warmth of your palm before the strike lands.
I brace, but not from fear.
I shiver, but not from cold.
I crave, but not just the pain—
I crave the moment before,
when the air is thick with expectation,
when my body is yours to command.

The first strike does not hurt.
Not truly.
It wakes me, pulls me deeper,
forces my focus into the present,
into you.
The second sears, the third lingers,
each a crescendo in a symphony only we can hear.

I arch, I writhe, I beg.
Not for it to stop,
but for it to continue,
for the burn, the sting, the ache—
for the proof of your power,
for the evidence of my surrender.

You watch me, study me,
learn my reactions,
adjust the rhythm, the force, the intensity.
You push, then pause,
give, then take,
and I respond like an instrument in your hands.

I exist in this space,
between pain and pleasure,
between discipline and reward,
between submission and the sharp, exquisite bliss
of knowing I would endure anything
to stay right here—beneath you.

The Final Surrender

It was never just about control,
never only about giving or taking.
It was about trust, about the space between us,
about the unspoken vow
that neither of us would break what we built here.

You have tested me, pushed me,
held me at the edge of pleasure and pain,
taught me the language of restraint,
the rhythm of surrender,
the art of knowing when to yield.

Every lesson has led to this—
this final moment,
where I no longer hold back,
where hesitation dissolves,
where submission is no longer something I do—
it is something I have become.

I feel it in your touch,
in the way your hands linger,
in the way your voice lowers,
commanding yet soft, firm yet careful.
You know what this means.
You know that this moment is not just an act—
It is the culmination of everything we are.

I do not resist.
I do not falter.
I give myself to you completely,
not just in body,
but in breath, in trust, in soul.
Not just in the way I kneel,
but in the way I let go.

This is the final surrender,
the deepest offering,
the moment where control and devotion merge into one.
And as you claim me,
as I fall into the space you have created for me,
I know with certainty—
I was always meant to be here.
Always meant to be yours.

I feel the weight of your hands upon me,
not just in touch but in presence,
in the power of knowing that I am truly seen,
truly held, truly understood.
You whisper my name,
not as a question but as an answer,
a reassurance that I have found my place.

And when the moment crests,
when the last barrier between us dissolves,
it is not just surrender that takes me—
it is freedom,
it is home,
it is love, wrapped in the promise of your control.

Acknowledgements

Writing a book is never a solitary endeavor, and I am deeply grateful to those who have supported me throughout this journey.

First and foremost, my heartfelt gratitude goes to **K**, the love of my life, whose unwavering belief in me made this book possible. Thank you for standing by my side, for your patience, encouragement, and for allowing me to be unapologetically myself. This journey would not have been the same without you.

To my family and friends, thank you for your constant love, understanding, and support. Your encouragement kept me going, even on the most challenging days.

A special thank you to **James & Larissa**, whose early review of my poetry and encouragement helped shape this book into what it is today. Your belief in the messages within these pages gave me the confidence to see it through.

To my readers—whether you are discovering my work for the first time or have been with me for a while, thank you. Your support, enthusiasm, and love for storytelling inspire me every day.

Finally, to everyone who has been part of this journey, whether through a kind word, a piece of advice, or simply by believing in me—thank you. This book carries a piece of all of you within its pages.

With gratitude,
Raven Delacroix

About the Author

Raven Delacroix is a writer, poet, and unapologetic storyteller who delves into the raw, the intimate, and the untamed. With a passion for spoken word and slam poetry, her work explores themes of power, vulnerability, sensuality, and the beautifully dark complexities of human connection.

The BDSM Sessions is her debut collection—a fearless, evocative journey through the realms of dominance and submission, pain and pleasure, love and liberation. Her words are meant to be felt as much as they are read, igniting emotions that linger long after the final stanza.

She resides in Crossroads, Texas, where the quiet stillness of the night fuels her creativity. By her side is Nyx, her faithful Great Pyrenees/Catahoula mix, named after the primordial goddess of the night—a fitting companion for a writer who thrives in the shadows of poetry and prose.

When she's not writing, Raven finds inspiration in music, late-night conversations, and the art of pushing boundaries—both on the page and in life. She believes poetry should be immersive, raw, and unfiltered, just like the experiences that shape us.